Hairs · Pelitos

by Sandra Cisneros · illustrated by Terry Ybáñez

TRES FLORES

three flowers
BRILLIANTINE
CONTAINS:
3 ¾ OZ. NET WT.   PETROLATUM
FRAGRANCE

DRAGONFLY BOOKS ———→ NEW YORK

———————————————

Translated from the English by Liliana Valenzuela

Traducción al español por Liliana Valenzuela

Everybody in our family has different hair.

Todos en nuestra familia tenemos pelo diferente.

El pelo de mi papá es como una escoba,

all up in the air.

todo parado de punta.

And me, my hair is lazy.

Y yo, mi pelo es flojo.

It never obeys barrettes or bands.

Nunca obedece a broches o diademas.

Carlos's hair is thick and straight.

El pelo de Carlos es grueso y lacio.

He doesn't need to comb it.

No necesita peinárselo.

Nenny's hair is slippery—

El pelo de Nenny es resbaloso—

slides out of your hand.

se escurre de tu mano.

has hair like fur.

tiene pelo como peluche.

But my mother's hair, my mother's hair, like little rosettes,

Pero el pelo de mi mamá, el pelo de mi mamá, como rositas,

like little candy circles, all curly and pretty because

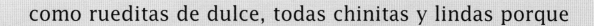
como rueditas de dulce, todas chinitas y lindas porque

she pinned it in pin curls all day,

se hizo anchoas con pasadores todo el día,

sweet to put your nose into when she is holding you,

dulce cuando pones tu nariz en él cuando ella te abraza,

holding you and you feel safe,

cuando te abraza y te sientes segura,

is the warm smell of bread before you bake it,

es el olor tibio a pan antes de hornearlo,

is the smell when she makes room for you

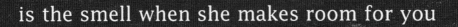

es el olor cuando te hace un campito

on her side of the bed still warm with her skin,

en su lado de la cama todavía calientito de su piel,

and you sleep near her,

y te duermes cerca de ella,

the rain outside falling and Papa snoring.

la lluvia cayendo afuera y Papá roncando.

The snoring, the rain, and Mama's hair that smells like bread.

Los ronquidos, la lluvia, y el pelo de Mamá que huele a pan.

All rights reserved. Published in the United States by Dragonfly Books, an imprint of
Random House Children's Books, a division of Random House, Inc., New York. The text of this work
was originally published as part of the collection *The House on Mango Street,* by Arte Publico Press, Houston, in 1984.
Published in hardcover in the United States by Alfred A. Knopf, an imprint of Random House Children's Books,
a division of Random House, Inc., New York, in 1994.

Dragonfly Books with the colophon is a registered trademark of Random House, Inc.

Visit us on the Web! www.randomhouse.com/kids

Educators and librarians, for a variety of teaching tools, visit us at
www.randomhouse.com/teachers

The Library of Congress has cataloged the hardcover edition of this work as follows:

Cisneros, Sandra.
Hairs = Pelitos / by Sandra Cisneros ; illustrated by Terry Ybáñez.
p. cm.
Summary: A child describes how each person in the family has hair that looks and
acts different, Papa's like a broom, Kiki's like fur, and Mama's with the smell of warm bread.
ISBN 978-0-679-86171-3 (trade) — ISBN 978-0-679-96171-0 (lib. bdg.)
[1. Hair—Fiction. 2. Hispanic Americans—Fiction. 3. Spanish language materials—Bilingual.]
I. Ybáñez, Terry, ill. II. Title. III. Title: Pelitos.
PZ73.C53   1994   93032775

ISBN 978-0-679-89007-2 (pbk.)

MANUFACTURED IN CHINA
33 32 31

Dragonfly Books introduce children
to the pleasures of caring about and sharing books.
With Dragonfly Books, children will discover
talented artists and writers and
the worlds they have created,
ranging from first concept books to
read-together stories to books for
newly independent readers.

One of the best gifts a child can receive
is a book to read and enjoy.
Sharing reading with children today
benefits them now and in the future.

Begin building your child's future . . .
one Dragonfly Book at a time.

For help in selecting books, look for these themes
on the back cover of every Dragonfly Book:

CLASSICS (Including Caldecott Award Winners)
CONCEPTS (Alphabet, Counting, and More)
CULTURAL DIVERSITY
DEATH AND DYING
FAMILY
FASCINATING PEOPLE
FRIENDSHIP
GROWING UP
JUST FOR FUN
MYTHS AND LEGENDS
NATURE AND OUR ENVIRONMENT
OUR HISTORY (Nonfiction and Historical Fiction)
POETRY
SCHOOL
SPORTS

Praise for
Hairs ⟲ Pelitos

"An affectionate picture of familial love, and a cozy bedtime book." —*The Horn Book Magazine*

"A spirited, buoyant celebration of individuality and of the bonds within families." —*Publishers Weekly*

From Papa's stiff brush cut to Kiki's bushy cap, like fur, to Nenny's slippery locks, here's a family with all different kinds of hair. And then there's Mama, whose hair smells sweet like bread. Mama's hair is like no one else's.

This jewel-like vignette from Sandra Cisneros's bestselling *The House ⬤* celebrates one loving family—in all its diversity.

Desde el corte de pelo tipo cepillo de papá, hasta la espesa cabellera de Ki⬤ baloso de Nenny, ésta es una familia con todo tipo de pelo. Y luego esta mama, cuyo pelo tiene un olor dulce como el pan. El pelo de mamá es único e incomparable.

Este maravilloso retrato de una familia unida, en toda su diversidad, proviene del libro de Sandra Cisneros, *La Casa en Mango Street*, que tanto éxito ha tenido.

A *Parenting* Magazine Best Book of the Year

DRAGONFLY BOOKS allow children to think . . . to imagine . . . to dream.

The theme of this book is:

CULTURAL DIVERSITY

Need help choosing books your child will enjoy again and again?
Look for other books with this theme:

LOOK INSIDE FOR MORE THEMES!

www.randomhouse.com/kids MANUFACTURED IN CHINA

US $7.99 / **$8.99 CAN**

ISBN 978-0-679-89007-2

9 780679 890072   50799

DRAGONFLY BOOKS

DRAGONFLY BOOKS New York